# Monkey
### and
# Elephant

# Monkey and Elephant

Carole Lexa Schaefer

illustrated by Galia Bernstein

CANDLEWICK PRESS

To my forever friends, Connie and Marcia.
And to Waldo, who reads Elephant best.
C. L. S.

To Sheera
G. B.

Text copyright © 2012 by Carole Lexa Schaefer
Illustrations copyright © 2012 by Galia Bernstein

First paperback edition 2013

The Library of Congress has cataloged the hardcover edition as follows:

Schaefer, Carole Lexa.
Monkey and Elephant / Carole Lexa Schaefer ; illustrated by Galia Bernstein. —1st ed.
p. cm.
Summary: In three episodes two friends cool off on a hot day,
sing songs, and outsmart some riffraff wildcats.
ISBN 978-0-7636-4840-4 (hardcover)
[1. Monkeys—Fiction. 2. Elephants—Fiction. 3. Friendship—Fiction.]
I. Bernstein, Galia, ill. II. Title.
PZ7.S3315Mon 2012
[E]—dc22 2010050607

ISBN 978-0-7636-6261-5 (paperback)

12 13 14 15 16 17 SCP 10 9 8 7 6 5 4 3 2 1

Printed in Humen, Dongguan, China

This book was typeset in Triplex.
The illustrations were created digitally.

Candlewick Press
99 Dover Street
Somerville, Massachusetts 02144

visit us at www.candlewick.com

# Contents

# Chapter One
# GETTING A RIDE

Monkey and Elephant tried to rest under the afternoon sun.

"Ooh, too hot for me," said Monkey. She flopped to the ground.

1

"Me, too," said Elephant, fanning himself with his big ears. "What'll we do?"

Monkey sat up and scratched one pink ear. "How about we look for some shade trees?" she said.

3

"Okay," said Elephant. He swished his trunk. "Which way?"

Monkey spun around, then pointed. And off they set.

Monkey scampered.

Elephant galumped.

4

"Too fast. Too hot. Slow down," Monkey panted.

6

"No. Too slow," said Elephant.
"Hurry up."

Monkey plopped down on the dusty path. "How about giving me a ride?" she said.

"Okay," said Elephant. In one big swoop, he lifted Monkey onto his head.

"Ready, set, go!" called Monkey. And—bump, galump—away they went together.

After a while, Elephant asked, "How are you doing up there?"

"Too thirsty," said Monkey.

"Me, too," said Elephant, swishing his trunk. "What'll we do?"

"I see a puddle," said Monkey. "How about letting me down? I'll get us some water."

"Um, okay," said Elephant. He kept his trunk still.

Dip. Sip. Dip. Sip.

"Too little," said Elephant.

"My turn."

SNOOF. SPLASH.
SNOOF. SPLASH.

"Too much!" sputtered Monkey.

14

"No," said Elephant. "It makes us cool."

"Not anymore," said Monkey, drying off. "The puddle is gone."

## Chapter Two
# SINGING SONGS

"Elephant," said Monkey, "you are walking too bumpity."

"Sorry," said Elephant.

"And too ziggy, and too zaggy," said Monkey. "How about smoothing it out?"

"Humph,"
said Elephant.
"Too bossy."

"Too grumbly,"
said Monkey.

"Too *sassy*," said Elephant.

"Too *cranky*,"
said Monkey.

"Oh, dear," said Elephant, swishing his trunk. "What'll we do?"

"How about something we both like?" said Monkey. "Singing!"
"Good idea," said Elephant.

21

"Not too loud," said Monkey.

"Not too soft,"
said Elephant.

"I'll start," said Monkey.
Swinging along, they sang,

"Monkey
and Elephant,
under the too-hot sun,
look for a shady place to flop down
and snooze the hot, hot day . . .
AWAY-ay-ay!"

"Not *too* bad," said Monkey.

"How about singing some more?"

"Okay," said Elephant.

"You start this time," said Monkey.

25

"Great big Elephant
and quick little Monkey
bump galump along,
singing a super song
that is here to . . .
STAY-ay-ay!"

26

"That was fun," said Elephant.

"For sure," said Monkey. And she turned a little flip right on top of his head.

## Chapter Three
# FINDING SHAPES

"Look!" cried Monkey. "There are some shapes ahead. Could be trees."

"No," said Elephant. "Too short."

"True," said Monkey. "And way too jumpy."

Soon three riffraff wildcats were bouncing around them, yelling, "Did you know there is a monkey on your head?"

"Did you know monkey is a really good snack?"

"Did you know we are ready for a snack right now?"

Monkey tried to hide behind Elephant's big ears. "Too *scary!*" she squealed. "What'll we do?"

Elephant puffed out his cheeks
and hollered, "QUIET!"
The wildcats sat still.

Elephant scuffed up the ground.
"How about," he said, "you guys
have DUST CAKE for snack today?"

With Monkey holding on tight,
Elephant stomped away.

"Ooh, look," said Monkey. "More shapes ahead."

"Are they moving?" said Elephant.

"No," said Monkey. "They are trees!"

"For sure?" said Elephant.

"For sure," said Monkey. She clapped her hands.

Resting in the shade, Monkey said, "Elephant, you are strong and brave and kind."

"Thanks," said Elephant. He closed his eyes.

"What about me?" said Monkey. "You are, um, bouncy," said Elephant. "And you are spunky and smart."

39

"Thanks," said Monkey. "I like you, Elephant."

"Good," said Elephant.

"Not too much," said Monkey.

"What?" said Elephant. He opened his eyes.

"And not too little," said Monkey.

"Oh," said Elephant.

"I like you just right," said Monkey.

"Ahh," sighed Elephant. "Me, too."